When I Can't Sleep

a collection of flash fiction

Robert Garner McBrearty

MATTER PRESS
Wynnewood, Pennsylvania

First Matter Press Edition, 2019

ISBN: 978-0-9961558-5-4

Cover design by Roma Narkhede
Interior design concept by HR Hegnauer
Text set in Bembo

MATTER PRESS
PO Box 704
Wynnewood, PA 19096
www.matterpress.com

WHEN I CAN'T SLEEP

INTRODUCTION

I like reading flash fiction and long Russian novels, though I am not likely to write anything resembling a long Russian novel. I like writing and reading longer short stories, too, but when I pick up a literary magazine or an anthology, I find myself flipping through it to find the shortest story. The novels of Dostoyevsky and Tolstoy are wonderful in their own ways, but there are times when I can't wait, when I want all the life and beauty that can be found in one or two pages. Think of poetry for a moment, the way a few great lines can transport us and stick with us all our lives: *Do not go gentle into that good night...I wake to sleep and take my waking slow...*

Some flash fiction comes, well, in a flash. Many of these stories came to me in that space that exists between sleeping and waking, as if a voice were whispering the first lines, a scenario unfolding. Some ideas made me sit up in bed. If the ideas tugged at me enough, I'd get up and write them down. No doubt others were lost because I didn't get up to write them down.

Some of these stories were written in a flash, a sort of gallop across the page, and if they came too easily, I might allay my guilt by saying it's like a wrestling match, which takes only a few minutes in real time but which is amazingly strenuous and one must consider the countless hours of training, of grueling workouts, before the wrestler walks out on the mat. Others took many years once they were first drafted. The balance must be just right. A small rock under a wheel can send a bike careening. And yet, a ride with no surprises is boring. One wants the moment of wonder before regaining balance.

Before this moment in time flashes on, my thanks and love to my wife and children, friends and family.

When I Can't Sleep

a collection of flash fiction

DOWN AT AL'S POOL HALL

I keep waiting for good news. But no one calls. No one knocks on the door. Maybe tomorrow.

We're all sleepy here in our town. We slog around in the summer heat, waiting for something to happen. At night, I open the window of my furnished room and lie in the heat and hear the town buzzing like a fat, lazy bee.

My friends here lack gumption, lack get up and go. Some went to college, some didn't, but we're all stuck in dead-end jobs, or no jobs at all. We hang out at Al's Pool Hall and all we talk about are girls, but the girls are sick and tired of waiting for us to come out of Al's Pool Hall and do something with our lives besides drink and play pool.

It was different when Al was still here. He gave us pep talks, told us to go out in the world, to expand our horizons, to find our dream, to do more with our lives than our parents had. If someone was down on his luck, Al was always there to listen. If we were out walking, he'd drive by in his big red pick-up and honk and wave. Just seeing him cheered us up, gave us a sense of purpose. There's Al, we'd say, let's go see Al.

On one of his adventures, to a game refuge this time, he sent back pictures and cheerful and inspiring articles for the local newspaper. One night, a lion broke into his tent and clamped Al's head in its teeth. It dragged him out of the tent and into the brush. But we know that through it all, Al would have kept his upbeat attitude. This happens all the time, he would have told himself. They maul you a little and move on.

We still hang out at the pool hall, but we're lost without Al. The new manager chews us out if we hang out without spending much or if we get too loud. One night, Al's sister comes in and walks over to the pool table where we're playing. They used to live together, brother and sister. She starts crying, so I put my arms around her and hold her and she cries into my chest and tells me I was always one of Al's favorites.

A couple of days later, there's an envelope in my mailbox. I open it and there's a key inside and a message on white unlined paper that says: *Al's pick-up. Take it and go. Find your dream. You'll need to recharge the battery.*

I'm already packing. I won't leave much behind. Tomorrow I'll drive Al's pick-up down to the pool hall. I'll honk for the guys to come out. No more waiting around. I'm leaving town. Anyone who wants can come with me.

WHAT HAPPENED TO LAURA?

I'm in a coffee shop on a spring afternoon when a man at a table near the creamers picks up his smart phone and says in a loud voice, "John? Doug here. Laura is back. She's pissed off. She's a really pissed off person...I don't know what she's pissed off about...Yeah, that's right...I'm taking her into the doctor today...It's a hard call, they might... That's good, that's good...She's real angry, she's real brutal, she's real cutting...Yeah, that's right...I don't know if I'm going to have to hospitalize her or not...It's brutal, it's real brutal, I'll call you after we see the doctor...Okay, thanks, right...That's good."

Doug signs off. But he's back on a moment later. "Bob? Doug here. Laura came back...Well, she's pissed off. She's real pissed off...We're going to see the doctor in about twenty minutes...Obviously...Excellent...Good idea...I'll hide everything."

He hangs up. We all look up from our tables to meet his widened eyes. A tall man rises. He points a finger at Doug's chest. "I want to know what's wrong with Laura," he says.

A woman in a leather jacket turns from the pastry display. "Maybe she has good reasons to be pissed off."

We nod. "Yeah," we say as one, "we want to know what's wrong with Laura."

Doug's eyes twitch. His brow crinkles in alarm.

"I don't want Laura to get screwed over," the woman in the leather jacket says.

"Talk to us, Doug," the tall man says. "Make it easy for

everybody."

The barista, a young man with dragon tattoos on his forearms, comes out from behind the bar and sets a steamy cup in front of the man. It looks loaded with all the hard stuff, maybe a double mocha. He breathes over the man. "Maybe this will loosen your lips," he says.

Doug shrinks back in his seat, hand on his phone. We lean in on him.

"It's Laura I'm concerned about," the woman says.

"Of course you are," we say. "We all are."

THE ARMCHAIR

Moments after his wife has shot him and slammed the front door, leaving him alone in the kitchen, bleeding from his side, Samuels starts a slow painful walk toward his armchair in the living room. His cell phone is on the side table next to the chair and if he can make it there, he'll call 911 and take his shirt off and wrap it around the wound and rest on the armchair and wait for the paramedics. This is the third time he's been shot in his life and he knows it's a serious situation all right, but there's a good chance he can pull through this if the paramedics arrive in time. He hopes she hasn't locked the door as that will slow the medics down. He's never known her *not* to lock the door, but she's never shot him before either so it's a learning experience for both of them.

He cups his hand to his side and the blood slips through his fingers. Dripping blood across the kitchen floor, noticing the cracked yellow linoleum, damn, should have replaced that years ago, he walks heavy-legged toward the brown armchair and he is reminded of the back surgery he had as a young man coming back from the war when a male nurse got in his face and told him he had to walk if he was going to get better but it hurt so bad he couldn't even make it across the room before begging to lie back down, and then later there was another surgery in another hospital and he was in bed and his wife was trying to press a spoonful of foul gray soup through his clamped lips and making little *eat, baby noises* to encourage him and he cursed at her and slapped the spoon out of her hand and she jumped back like he'd struck her.

As he gets close to the armchair, the pain is mostly gone, turned to a strange numbness in his side that's spreading down his legs. He comes to a halt, his eyes traveling beyond the armchair. He gazes through the window into his back yard, mesmerized by the autumn sky, the high limbs of the trees shadowing his house.

A bird flies past the window and he follows it with his eyes. He blinks, resettles his gaze on the armchair, clanks forward with jerking steps. It's a big brown armchair with wide welcoming arms. His wife had picked it out for them in happier days, and they'd made love on that armchair, her legs sticking up over his shoulders in that great flexible way she had. They had been happy once and it's a shame that instead of working things out, all she could think to do was shoot him. But as he sinks into the softness and depth of the armchair, he's cautiously optimistic because she's a good shot and he knows she could have killed him if she had wanted.

THE IMITATION

They had just finished making love, a rousing session, and Sullivan worried that his fiancé had been so loud that their neighbors in the house to their left, the closest house to their bedroom window, might have heard her. It was nearly midnight and the neighborhood was quiet other than the summery sound of crickets, birds, the drone of an air conditioner, a train passing in the distance. The couple next door had a neat lawn and two small children. The man in particular was rather standoffish. The most Sullivan could get out of him was a quick wave if they happened to cross paths. He thought perhaps the man thought ill of them because they were renters rather than owners, because their lawn was not so neat, and because they had no children. It was a neighborhood of small ranch houses with neat yards and there were lots of children roaming about. He worried that he and his fiancé stood out somehow and this man next door would think even more poorly of them if he heard the lovemaking and he might spread the news around so that everyone in the neighborhood would make fun of them and then maybe some of the kids who were a little older would sneak over one night and toilet-paper their trees. When he had been in middle-school, he had not been very popular and one night the family house had been toilet-papered and his parents blamed him for it and he had felt ashamed for several months afterward, both by this mark of his own unpopularity and by his parents' recognition of his unpopularity.

As they lay in bed, he mentioned to his fiancé, tactfully he thought, that maybe she should be a little quieter in the future so that the neighbors would not hear her. I wasn't that loud, she said, God, the window was closed, and who cares what the neighbors think?

I'll tell you what, Sullivan said. How about if I stand outside the bedroom window and you make the same noises you were making, and I will listen and see if I hear you. I'll tap on the window to tell you to stop the moment I hear something.

That's crazy, she said, I'm not going to do that. I would feel really stupid doing that.

Okay, then, how about if you go outside and I will make the noises and you can listen and tap on the window if you hear me?

God, this is sick, she said. Fine. Whatever.

Tap on the window when you arrive.

She threw on a robe and went huffily into the night. He waited until he heard the tap on the window. He started quietly at first, making little moans and sighs. There was no tapping. By degrees he became louder and now he added in little endearments and the sort of encouragements she would use like oh, that's wonderful, right there, there! Bring it on now! There was still no tapping so he really belted it out for some more minutes, imitating her sounds.

Finally he stopped. She came back in a minute later. Her face was dark and scowling.

Well? he asked, nothing? I guess we're okay then.

She got back in bed in her robe. She lay turned away

from him, keeping as far away in the bed as she could.

Shortly after, she broke up with him and they both abandoned the neighborhood. For years after, he missed her. He thought of her sounds as something beautiful that had been forever lost to him. His lover now was utterly silent.

IN THE BLACKNESS

When he woke in the blackness, heart pounding, he knew instantly that he had been buried alive. What a bunch of imbeciles!

He'd been shot twice, but he knew that he had a good chance of survival when he staggered bleeding into the emergency room. Just his luck to get a crew of incompetents who couldn't handle a couple of simple shots to the guts. He'd had a feeling going under that they were going to screw up.

And boy had they, royally! The dumb clucks had had him buried alive.

He'd have to think about this. This wasn't going to be an easy one. First off, he realized that he had no use of his hands. He sent signals to his hands and arms, willed them to move, but nothing. Obviously, they'd laid on the meds too thick. He supposed he could kick the lid of the coffin off, but no luck there. The legs weren't working either.

He wasn't uncomfortable. He had a pleasant floating sensation. He wasn't short of air. So that was good. He didn't feel particularly worried – in fact, after the first surprise, his heart had settled right down. Maybe they hadn't screwed up as badly as he had thought. They must have him in some sort of pressurized chamber and it was just a matter of waiting.

He didn't feel especially impatient, and he had often been an impatient man. Classical music was playing from somewhere and he found it very pleasant. He had never set aside time to listen to classical music, but now and then when he heard it, especially the violins, the music swept over him like a wave, called forth memories and dreams, and sometimes it was difficult to tell what was memory and what was dream.

Too soon, though it was difficult to say what was soon or late, the violins faded away and were replaced by gunfire. The team was in a firefight in the jungle, and there were rockets coming in, an explosion, and the shrapnel tore into them and he heard screams. He put his face to the ground, smelled the earth, tasted it on his lips, for the last time maybe, then that scene faded away and the team had been sent to another planet, which was dry, pitted, moon-like, the air bitter and acrid, desolate, sad somehow.

He and Davey and Hammer and Rotter were in a shallow ditch, taking heat from creatures that were like humans, except more waxy and fatty.

They were moving in closer and he said, "Toss a couple of grenades at them, Davey."

"Grenades! Yeah, man!" Davey tended to get too excited, but you could depend on him with your life.

"Hoo-yah!" Hammer said. There was something oafish and crude about Hammer. He would have broken off from Hammer long ago, but Hammer and Davey were close.

"Maybe we could hit them with a little hippo juice instead," Rotter said. He was always the tactful one, the negotiator.

Yeah, that's right, that was the newest thing, the hippo juice. Came out of a canister, like a flamethrower sort of, but a gas, a harmless one, made soldiers move around slow like hippos, thus the name. They'd wobble and fall over and sleep, but they'd wake up okay. It was a more humane way of doing things.

"Sure," he said, though Davey and Hammer were disappointed. "Use the hippo juice instead of the grenades." Why not? Why kill anybody if they didn't have to? He was already haunted by the dead. He didn't need to add any more to the toll.

Sure enough, the creatures staggered around, moving slow like hippos on a landscape that looked even more lunar now than it had moments ago.

"How about now we hit 'em with the grenades!" Hammer said.

"No. No grenades. Let's clear out." This was okay now, for once they weren't leaving dead bodies in their wake.

Flight, light, darkness, speeding, slowing, and now they traveled on trains and buses and then through long corridors, and elevators up and down, and along moving walkways and through metal doors into rooms with questioners and lights and doctors probing them, and the team was released back into the city, walking city streets, restless, calling each other at all hours, the team calling him and crying sometimes for reasons they could never say, and they had found this new business, found they were good at it, but this robbery wasn't going well. He'd had a bad feeling about it. He'd told Marcia it was his last job, and he'd meant it too, but maybe telling her, planning it to be the last, had set off some bad luck.

The bank teller was agitated, hands fumbling, slow with

the money. Then they knew he'd pressed the alarm. You always knew when that happened. It was to be expected and you had to plan your timing accordingly.

But this time Hammer lost it, sprayed Uzi fire everywhere like he was in a bad movie, the panicked, screaming customers and tellers diving to the marble floor. He wasn't even sure how many had been hit, and Hammer was still firing when he stepped up to him and pressed his gun to his temple and pulled the trigger. Hammer's knees went out and he dropped.

He'd killed Hammer. He'd killed Hammer, stupid Hammer.

Davey stared at him in disbelief. Then Davey, his best friend in all the world, shot him, shot him twice. Rotter was looking on, in horror, and trying to move between them when Davey shot him, too, maybe by accident, maybe not, and Rotter stumbled for a moment, slowly, as if he'd been hit with the hippo juice, then fell. Out the door of the bank he ran bloodied with Davey after him now, Davey, his best friend in all the world firing at him, but then Davey breaking away, the both of them alone to make their own way.

He heard the music again, more distantly, and he was happy now because he was with Marcia. They were dancing in an elegant ballroom, but they had the ballroom to themselves. She smiled. She had such a lovely smile, her hair so dark. They danced in the elegant, empty ballroom.

Later, this must have been later, they had two children, a lovely boy and a lovely girl. They lived peacefully. The children were happy.

They danced in the ballroom. Somewhere there were children. They lived in a country home. They had a white horse. No one rode the horse. But they liked to go out and feed the horse carrots. The horse liked the carrots and the horse was always happy to see them.

They walked in the countryside with his arm around her. Sometimes the children were there and sometimes they were not.

He would shut his eyes now and wait.

THE OLD RED DOG

Our dog Jeeter was a big, terrible, red-furred bastard, and when I was a kid it would knock me down and bite me on the ass.

When my brother and I left home, our mother made us take Jeeter with us. He got meaner every year. The dog lived to be twenty and its hair fell out and blisters and orange scabs formed on its back. On the day he died, Jeeter bit me on the ass and then keeled over and rolled down the stairs.

After the dog died, my brother and I buried it in our yard. Then we got drunk and we rolled around on the carpet, hitting each other. Our older brother, the doctor, came over and found us rolling around on the carpet. He called us worthless pieces of shit and stormed out. We didn't even have time to tell him Jeeter had died. He was always showing up, calling us worthless pieces of shit, and then storming out. I think it was therapeutic for him.

That night, we dug the dog back up and drove over to our brother's place and left the body on his front porch. He had always hated that dog. He'd never wanted anything to do with that dog.

He came over the next morning, crying. I didn't know Jeeter had died, he said. I loved that old dog. We all got drunk and we buried Jeeter again, in a deeper and a better grave.

THE GARDENER

Standing in the garden, I fired at my head, but my hand was shaking and I jerked the barrel upwards so that the bullet flew over my head and into the trees beyond. I was deafened from the blast so when the gardener came out of the shed carrying the spade, I had to punch at my ears a few times until I finally made out his shout.

"What are you doing?" he demanded. He wasn't your usual kindly, earth-loving gardener. He was mean, lanky with sharp elbows. He was always yanking at the bushes and speaking angrily to the shrubs. I'd seen him whack with an ax at a fruit tree.

"I wasn't doing anything," I said. "Trying to shoot myself, I guess."

"This early in the morning? You'll be waking everyone." He took the gun out of my hand, tucked it into the pockets of his overalls. "That's just like you. Not worried about the way you inconvenience others."

"Sorry," I said. "I guess I was just in despair."

"Despair," he scoffed. "Despair. That's a big word for the likes of you. Despair, my ass."

He poked me with the spade. I leaped to the side and he followed, jabbing at me with the spade, forcing me backwards towards the shed. I tried to dodge the jabbing spade, but I was ringed in by Bonzai bushes. "March, you," he said. "March." He prodded me along, backing me into the shed. He gave me a final push into a dark corner. "I'll give you something to despair about," he said as he locked me in.

It was cool and dim in there and it smelled of clay and mulch. I could hear the sound of earth moving and the heavy trod of his boots. By and by my breathing slowed, and I thought that one might do worse than spending the day in a cool, dark shed.

I heard the unlocking of the door and the light flooded my eyes.

"Out, you," he said.

He was carrying a shovel now, and he gestured with it but did not poke me as he led me across the garden where he'd dug a deep hole.

"Well," he said. "Is it good enough for you? Will it do?"

He reached into the depths of his overalls, brought forth the gun and handed it over to me. He gave me an encouraging nod. "I can bury you right up now. Nice and neat."

I stood there, frowning, turning the gun in my hand.

"It's no bother now that I've got the hole," he said. "Earlier, I wasn't sure where I'd put you, but this should work nicely now."

"But I've changed my mind," I said, trying to hand the gun back to him, "I don't want to shoot myself after all."

He pushed the gun back toward me, forcing me to take it. "Come on, now," he said. "Don't talk nonsense. I can give you a little privacy if you'd like. I'll just step behind the bushes for a bit, and if you stand right here, you should fall right into the hole."

"I'm sorry," I said. "I won't be needing the hole."

He stood back, his hands tightening on the handle of the shovel. His chin stretched toward me and sharpened a notch. "Oh, you're a fine one," he said. "All that effort to dig you a nice hole, and now you tell me you won't be needing it?"

"I'm afraid not. I've changed my mind." I tossed the gun deep into the bushes. "Sorry."

He threw down the shovel. "After all that digging? That's it? Sorry?" He lowered himself into the hole and lay down on the muddy earth. He folded his hands over his chest. "Just bury me," he said. "You know you've always wanted to!"

I kicked a little dirt in on his face to make him happy, and then I had the shovel in my hands and I was throwing the earth in as fast as I could to cover up the mean old bastard. As he sputtered and wiped the dirt from his face, I tossed the shovel aside. "That's it," I said, "We're done." I left him crying out from his fine hole, "No gratitude at all! Not a word of thanks!"

As I took off running, his bellowing voice followed me, a mix of ancient fury and lamentation, but I kept on running without looking back, and I've been running ever since.

SEND NOW

This was the big one, the one Chuck had dreamed of all these years–the great story after all the years of being kicked around by the brutal establishment magazines. It had it all–a lost dog, a lonely pony, an orphan, a dyslexic actor, and a ballerina with a bum foot all in one story. And all he had to do now was hit the Send button.

It was late afternoon now and he'd worked all day. Now he had the attachment all set and he'd already addressed the cover letter to the major magazine, *the* major magazine, oh yeah, *the* major magazine that had rejected every story of his for thirty years and counting, but *this* was the one that would make the editors weep and apologize for not discovering his work earlier.

Not that he was bitter. Not now! He would savor the moment before hitting the Send button, so he went into his kitchen for another cup of coffee. He added the milk and sugar. He usually avoided sugar since his health problems had started, but sugar *definitely* was called for this time. He stirred in the sugar, finding a kind of beauty in the slow circular motion of his hand as he stirred. It was a fine hand. The hand of a writer, a little bruised around the knuckles, the flesh at the fingertips worn from beating the keyboard.

He sipped. *Ah*, he sighed. When he had been a college teacher, he'd had a little ritual. He'd stand before his desk and raise his cup to his lips and let out a mighty sigh: *Ah*. The students enjoyed the moment. They'd watch him. Ah, he'd sigh. They'd laugh and then class would get underway.

His wife, Julie, a nurse, had gone in early to the hospital and she would be home soon. He recalled now that he used to have his *Ah* moments with her, too. After finishing a story, he would get his coffee and look at her and pose with his cup and sip and let out a big *Ah*. That was in the better days when she still cared about his stories, when she still cared about *him*. But there had been distance in recent years, distance as all the rejections and disappointments weighed upon her as well as him. For the last months, he hadn't even let her read his stories, not after she'd described one of his stories as "gibberish." Well, *exactly*! The story had been about a guy who is going mad and writing gibberish, so the fact that the story did in fact sound like gibberish was a sign that he had *succeeded*! But she had failed to appreciate the finer point.

Well, his relationship with Julie would soon be turned around. She would believe in him again! And if not, well, the women would be lining up in droves after the story appeared in *the* major magazine. Oh yeah, there would be plenty of women, don't worry about *that*!

He went down the short hallway, triumph and joy rising in his chest like a wave, but halfway down the hallway, the rising joy in his chest turned to a surging heat wave and he collapsed to his knees and sprawled on the floor, the *Ah* cup of coffee spilling out before him. His heart exploding, he crawled toward the computer. *Must hit the Send button.* As he faded he was comforted in knowing Julie would know what to do. She would preserve his legacy. She would hit the Send button.

When she came home in the afternoon and found

Chuck in the hallway, Julie did not panic. She went into her "cool safe" zone as a nurse. She could tell right away, but she checked his pulse anyway. Yup, sure enough, he was dead. No doubt about it. Totally dead. This was going to be a pain in the ass, notifying people, arranging the funeral. She was in no rush to deal with all that. She made herself a cup of coffee in the kitchen, sipped, let out a bit of an "Ah" and walked back down the hallway, stepped over Chuck's body, avoided the spilled coffee–what a mess!–and went into the office to the computer.

She saw the cover letter to the editor, opened the attachment. Chuck had been talented once. She'd believed in him, but as the years had rolled by without much to show for it, they'd both grown disillusioned. She recalled one recent story that was absolute *gibberish.*

She started to read Chuck's story and her eyes teared up. My God, this one was beautiful. The sad pony! The stumbling ballerina! The actor who mixed up his lines. Opening his other files now, skimming through them, she saw that there were really quite a few good unpublished stories there. Sending them out would keep her busy for some time and help her deal with the grief, which she knew might begin after she left her cool, safe zone. After all there had been some good years together before the long bleak period settled in.

She saw that the story was aimed at the big one, *the* major magazine as Chuck would say, the grand cabana, the big cheese, the ring to rule them all. These were sensitive, beautiful stories, not really suited to an author named Chuck. *Julie.* Yes, that would be a good writer's name going forward.

She made the right change and hit the Send button.

INTO THE BASEMENT

As we walk on the nearly empty outdoor mall on an early Sunday morning, Christmas coming on soon, no snow today, but cold in the air, my wife's shoulder bumps mine and we both teeter a bit and she says, "This is really bad. We're both having nervous breakdowns at the same time."

"I know, I know," I say, "don't worry about it, move on."

"We're only doing this because we're crazy," she says, "you know that."

"Of course I know that, what do you think I am, crazy?" I look ahead and to the side and see a man huddled against a storefront wall, a blanket over his shoulders. His breath comes out in white puffs in the air. "Look, there's one there. Grab him."

"Jesus," she says, "that's not the right approach. Invite him."

"Hell, I don't know if it's such a great invitation. It's just a lousy basement."

At first we just gave the street people food, but we're upping our game. We have some resources that we might as well use since our own children are grown and gone and doing well on their own. They live far off across the country. They don't visit much. Sometimes they call or send an email. We were on Facebook with them for a while, but I think they unfriended us. Maybe we need somebody who needs us. We have a big basement and the homeless shelter is full, so we're letting some of the homeless crash for the winter.

"Maybe we'd better pass on this one," my wife says. "We have ten now. What if they become unhappy with the basement? I heard shuffling around last night."

We have friends who have warned us we'll be robbed or murdered if we're not careful. But our visitors are friendly people. They like it when we bring down breakfast and fresh towels. But we keep them in the basement. "Don't worry. I'll shoot them if they come up the stairs."

"God!" she says. "Don't say that! Are you nuts! This is all because we feel guilty."

"We have too much."

"We could just give it away."

"Then we would have nothing to give away. We're selfish. We like having something to give away."

"Maybe there's a better way of doing it."

"We're old. We'll probably be dead by this time next year anyway. And I still can't decide whether I want to be buried or cremated."

"God, would you stop saying depressing things like that!"

"Sorry. Maybe I haven't had enough coffee this morning."

"If you would just for once stop saying these depressing things."

"Okay, okay. Cremation or burial are both fine with me. Whatever works for you. I want to make it as easy on you as possible."

"Forget it. Let's go invite him."

Side by side, we steer our bodies toward him and stand over the fellow. A cold wind blows against our backs and we almost topple over on him. He looks up, a stoical expression turning frightened. He's been left in the cold too long.

"What's your name?" we ask.

His eyes go wide. He lifts and spreads his empty hands as if it's a tough question.

"I know," I say, "I know. I can hardly remember my own."

"Stop it," my wife says. "Do you want the man to think we're crazy?"

"We want to offer you a place in our basement," I say. "Just until the weather warms up. It will be a little crowded. There are already some others down there."

His lips tremble. "You know my name."

"We do?"

He stands, raising himself on creaky knees, adjusting the blanket like a serape thrown over his shoulder, giving him a faintly Western gunslinger look. Now that he's standing he looks younger than I first thought, in his early thirties. "I lived in that basement."

"You did?"

"I'm Jeffrey. Your son. You almost killed me off in that hell hole. You forgot about me down there and let me rot. Fuck your basement."

He stumbles away, a certain weaving dignity to his steps. We watch him all the way to the corner, crossing the street to the next section of mall.

My spine tingles. My wife's shoulder jitters against mine.

I stare after the man, though he's already disappearing behind some trees on the mall. I lick my dry lips, set my brow in thought. "We didn't have a son named Jeffrey, did we?"

She breathes out hard. "Stop it! Of course not. Do you want me to think you're losing your marbles?"

I take her elbow. "Let's head home." My steps are determined now, forceful, I know where we are and what we are doing. A winter's sun shines brightly. "Of course we didn't have a son named Jeffrey," I say. "Of course I knew that."

The mall is beginning to pick up with people now, more morning strollers, a street magician preparing his gear for the show. We have seen his show before. He can swallow a whole burning sword and pull it out his ass.

A sudden wind blows dead leaves across our path, the swirling taking us by surprise. We fall against each other. "We didn't, did we?" Her voice is rushed, anxious. "Tell me we didn't."

"We didn't."

She's near tears. "It's not a hell hole. It wasn't. Our children were happy. Weren't they? *Weren't they*?"

THE STORY OF YOUR LIFE

The fellow sitting next to me at the bar said, "I went through some rough times. You ought to write the story of my life."

"I will, John," I said, 'I'll do it right now."

In those days, I always carried pen and paper with me, and as John told me his story, I wrote: *John Springer was born in a small town in Ohio. His father passed away when he was fifteen, and his mother shortly after, and nobody figured out that John was living in the old house alone. He ate what was left in the fridge, and then he turned to cannibalism. He first took down his neighbor, Joe, across the street...*

John leaned in. "What do you got so far?"

I read what I'd written and his eyes widened. "This is all wrong. I wasn't born in Ohio. A cannibal!"

"It's interpretive, John. This is the descent part. You need the descent before the redemption."

"You son of a bitch! You've made a mockery of my life!" He threw his drink in my face and struck me. We grappled at the bar as I tried to ward him off. The bartenders forced us out on the street. He went off howling down the block. "You've ruined my life!" he shouted.

"Come back, John," I cried. "I love you. I love your life!"

But he went on, bellowing in outrage. I can't stand to be alone. I want to tell your story.

THE BRIEFCASE

My wife always worried that I would forget to take my briefcase. As I'd go out the door of the house, she would call: Don't forget your briefcase.

Day after day, I lugged this thing across campus. It was a black cloth briefcase. It had straps and I could sling it over my shoulder if I wanted, though I rarely did. In most of my years teaching, I carried it by the hand grip. I liked carrying it that way because it was heavy with my books and all the student papers, and I liked the arm exercise. But after many years of lugging the briefcase, one day I couldn't ignore how tired my arm felt, and from then on, I usually carried it over my shoulder.

When I was fifty-five or so, I was at a conference for teachers in a different city and I was talking to an old friend. I would only see him every few years at some sort of conference like this, but we knew each other well enough to talk easily. We sat at a table in a cafeteria drinking coffee, taking a break from the conference, from the relentless presentations, and he said something like: You know, the next ten years are going to be hard. I'm already bored with it.

I'm bored too, I had to admit.

I was giving a lecture the other day, he said, and I was bored silly. Just bored silly. I could hardly stand to listen to myself talk.

I know, I said, I know. I can't stand listening to myself either.

And yet, there were these ten years to pass. Of course,

it might be longer than that. But all I could picture was getting to sixty-five. I would not think beyond that.

I trudged on. Day after day. Carrying, lugging the briefcase. Slogging across campus, diving out of the way as the skateboarders, young rulers of the sidewalks, ran me off the paths that crossed the quadrangle. Sometimes I'd feel my back humped over, and I would have to make a conscious effort to stand up straighter. There was a bridge over a pond, and each time I paused on the bridge and thought of tossing my briefcase down into the lily-covered pond. Goodbye briefcase. Goodbye student papers. The papers seemed to have a life of their own, wiggling around inside the briefcase. Read us, the papers demanded. Fuck you, I said back, read yourselves.

But if I threw the briefcase into the pond, my wife would ask: Where is your briefcase? And because I did not like lying to her, I would have to say: I threw my briefcase into the pond. And this would not go over well. There would be a series of questions to answer. There would be a call to one of her therapist friends. My wife is a therapist herself, and at least sometimes she thinks of me as her patient as well as her husband. My wife is on top of things. She is young for her age. I liked to think that I was too, but there was this thing about the weight of the briefcase, the way it was getting heavier. I didn't want to tell her that even slung over my shoulder, the briefcase was getting heavier, because then there would be a call to her personal trainer.

So maybe I would have to lie after all, though I would not like doing so. I would have to think of some place the briefcase might be, or where I had lost it, I guess, since it wouldn't be returning. But then she would worry that I was becoming absent-minded, beyond what she already viewed as a problem, and she would call one of her doctor friends to see about some testing so maybe after all I would have to admit that I had thrown the briefcase into the pond.

So it was good that I didn't, though I thought about it each time I crossed over that bridge. I tried going different routes, but the bridge was the most direct route to and from class and I turned that way like an old horse plodding back to the stable.

The students wrote personal narratives. Mostly about ski trips. There'd be about three pages of waking up and dressing for the trip and being picked up by a couple of smart-alecky guys and maybe getting a cup of coffee and an Egg McMuffin—at least I could relate to the food—and on page four, the last page of the essay, the narrator would break his leg and as a result of the accident he would learn to live life more fully.

I suggested on one paper that the student forget about living life more fully and just focus on that Egg McMuffin. Just make the whole essay about that. The sudden joy of biting into a sandwich and swishing it down with a big gulp of coffee. I'd have the sun coming up and there you are with your two buddies in the car, with your leg to be broken soon, but put that on hold and let's just eat that sandwich.

Sometimes I thought maybe they ought to write about sex. I thought maybe they could write about that subject with more gusto. But probably it would just embarrass everybody and maybe get me fired. And then my wife would be calling a lawyer. The more I think about it, I'm glad they stuck to breaking their legs on ski trips.

Since retirement, I feel like I've stepped out of the world. And yet time's still going a little too fast. I'd like to slow it down even more. To lose all sense of time. To wander the neighborhood and look. Just look. To be in no hurry. To take it all in. But I worry there isn't all that much to take in. It's a pleasant neighborhood. The neighbors keep their small front lawns neat and clipped. The houses are neither new nor old, but something in-between. We live near what is called Old Town, and in Old Town the houses do indeed look old. Sometimes you can even see an old-timer sitting on a swinging bench on an old-looking porch. But I would not say this is always the case. Some of these old houses have vibrant young owners who swish in and out of front doors and they will look at you if you are walking by, if you happen to be lugging a cloth briefcase over your shoulder as you head to a coffee shop on Main Street. They will smile indulgently as if you are something out of the past, and it's all well and good that you are walking by here, but now, really, they need to get back to the serious business of ruling the world. But you'd better keep walking. You'd better make your way right to that coffee shop and be back in a reasonable amount of time, or the next thing you know your wife will be calling the police to find you and bring you home.

THE CARDBOARD DEER

She would like me to tell her all sorts of horrible things about myself, but there really isn't anything horrible to tell her, and if there were, I still wouldn't tell her. She thinks that if I tell her secrets about myself, I will be free of them, or at least I will learn to accept them. What rot. The truth is that if I can keep from telling her anything about myself, I will be more protected than ever. And protecting yourself is what it's all about.

My therapist works out of her home in an upstairs apartment. We're sitting on either end of a big lumpy couch, having a nice cup of tea in her nice bohemian den with its hanging ferns and an oriental carpet. She's a tall woman with a thin, long face and thick black hair. She's wearing a blue jean skirt and has her legs curled up beneath her as if I am simply a casual visitor. In our three months together, she has grown increasingly comfortable in my presence, and I would be quite comfortable too if it weren't for all the personal questions, which strike me as a little rude. But she's becoming frustrated because I have the good sense not to tell her anything personal about myself. We've been talking about my love life, or lack of one, and I've been telling her that it really doesn't matter, that I like being alone, and she starts asking me all sorts of nosy questions about my desires. I am attracted to my therapist and you should not tell people who you are attracted to anything personal about your desires. They may get the wrong idea about you. In these days of unbridled openness, I have some advice for you: do not be so eager to tell everyone everything about yourself.

We go from one thing to another. I shut her down in one subject area and she shifts to another, but she always leads the questions back to my parents.

Were you scared of your parents? she asks.

Oh no. They were very nice.

That is what I would tell anyone. It is not good to belittle your parents, especially if they have passed away. You should praise your parents up and down and take your lumps on the chin.

Did they fight a lot?

I can't remember them ever raising their voices. I'm pretty sure they never did.

They never shouted?

They never got mad. Especially my father. He never got mad.

They sound pretty restrained. Were they cold to you, to each other?

We didn't go around hugging all the time. We didn't need to.

What would you talk about?

The usual stuff.

Did you talk about sex?

Why would we talk about sex? Listen, my father was terrific. He taught me how to fish, to hunt, to box, to fix a fence, to build a fire, to remove my own appendix in an emergency, and if I can't do any of those things now, it's certainly not his fault.

What about your mother? What was she like?

She was even nicer than my father, if that is possible.

You know what I think? I think you're full of shit.

My therapist can be terribly blunt. She should get some help for that.

She wants to know why I can't breathe. Why I get these terrible attacks where I can't breathe. These attacks that sent me to her in the first place. She thinks that if I open up about myself, the attacks will stop. How wrong she is. And yet the attacks keep coming.

I am in my office one day and the people in my office think that our work is very urgent, and I feel that it is very urgent too, though I do not know why. But I assure you our work is urgent. It must be urgent because my heart beats fast the minute that I walk into the office and it beats fast all day long and it beats even faster as I drive home.

I am not frightened of the people in my office, and if I were, I would not tell you. I like everyone in our office. They have never done anything, not one little thing, ever, to make me feel unwanted, and if they had, I wouldn't tell you about it.

I never feel that my job is meaningless. It is too urgent to be meaningless. Sitting at my desk, I realize I am hot. It is as if a flame has started in my feet and has traveled up my legs and through my spine all the way to my cheeks and temples. I must have a drink of water. I walk to the water cooler and no one in the office looks up, and yet I know they are watching me. I want to cry out – I am hot! I want to scream at the top of my lungs, startle them as they fidget at their desks. But I would not be able to scream because my throat is thickening and squeezing shut. I sip the water and it goes down as if it has a long journey to make. And yet my throat is still parched. I wobble. Everyone in the office pauses as if they are considering looking up from their urgent work. But they do not look up. I go back to my desk. There are urgent matters. I must get my work out.

When are these attacks going to end?

Tell me about them.

I've told you. I can't breathe when they happen.

What goes on in your mind when they happen?

Nothing goes on in my mind.

But you worry that the people at work don't think you're doing a good job. You worry that they think you're incompetent.

I wouldn't say that.

Did your father make you feel incompetent?

Oh no. He was very patient.

Is that what you really think?

Well, he was busy, all right. He was busy. He would get a little brusque sometimes.

Well my God. He would get a little brusque. Imagine that.

Are you being sarcastic?

Three months and I've gotten out of you that your father would get a little brusque. We're making real headway. I guess I'll take what I can get...She leans forward a little...What would he do when he got brusque?

Who?

Your father. What would he do when he got brusque?

He would...He would just get brusque.

Why won't you trust me?

I look into her eyes, which are soft now and a little moist. She puts on a tough front, but she's too sensitive inside. She should get some help for that.

I must get my work out. It is urgent. At my desk, I begin to itch. But the itching isn't on the surface, but inside. Inside, I am breaking out in hives. I'm sweating. My throat is squeezing shut. I loosen my tie. Today the people in my office are finally, openly, all staring at me. If I can make it to the water cooler, I will be fine. I must not let the others know that I am breaking out in hives. I smile at them. I AM FINE. I pat my chest. Their faces loom in at me. I stumble for the water cooler. I topple to the floor. I must get up. It is urgent. Monsters lurk over me. Shout at me. Shout, shout, shout at me! What is wrong? Get the hell up!

If you could do anything, anything in the whole world, what would you do?

Take a good long nap.

If you could be anything, anything in the whole world, what would you be?

A doorman.

I want you to try something.

Okay.

I want you to visualize yourself as an animal. If you were an animal, what kind of animal would you be?

I would be an elephant.

An elephant? I don't picture you as an elephant.

Neither do I, frankly, but I would not tell her what kind

of animal I picture myself as. Telling people what kind of animal you picture yourself as can lead to a lot of trouble.

Give me another animal.

Cardboard.

Cardboard? What do you mean cardboard?

A cardboard deer.

Tell me about it.

There's nothing to tell. It just popped into my mind.

It's very interesting.

It's not. It doesn't mean anything. It didn't mean anything to me when I said it, and it doesn't mean anything to me now.

She lets out a long sigh. I don't think I can help you, she says. We're wasting our time.

I don't think so. I want to keep coming here. It's all I look forward to.

Why?

I feel the itching beneath my skin. I feel my breath high in my chest and the squeezing of my throat.

Because I love you.

My voice comes out hollow, the way a cardboard deer might sound. But after I say it, I am able to take a deep breath.

She sits on the other side of the couch, her eyes blinking. We can hear a lawnmower outside, the sound coming through the open window along with the summer breeze. We stare at each other. I open my hands. She stands. She smooths her skirt. She runs a hand through her thick black hair.

I'll get us some more tea, she says quietly.

Yes. Please.

Her skirt swishes as she goes into the kitchen. I swallow. I look down at my shoes. I should have polished them.

BRAZO IN THE NEW WORLD

Brazo has fallen hard from his horse. In his heavy armor, he struggles to a knee, adjusting the visor of his helmet. He peers through the narrow slot at the bodies of his friends sprawled in the sand. The sole survivor of the patrol, his eyes widen as the Indios, ten at least, maybe fifteen, feint toward him, dance back. They're jeering at the fallen warrior, waiting to see what he'll do. Not good, Brazo thinks, seriously not so good.

Though his men are dead and he is horseless and adrift in the New World, beset by the enemy, the odds of a painful death remarkably high, Brazo focuses on the good Spanish steel in his iron-gloved hand, this really first-rate sword, fashioned in Madrid, long and wide, but light enough for his strong hand.

Ha, then! They jump back as he rises to his full height, a big man, the biggest in his patrol, which, bitter to admit, is all dead now, and he swings the sword, pants *ha ha ha*, more like the sudden release of breath than like laughter. For the moment, the swinging of the big sword keeps the ones in front of him in check. The problem is with the ones slipping behind.

He wheels about, nimble for an armored man, and faces the assailants on this side, long sword in one hand, short sword in the other. An arrow bounces off his armor and he swells with pride for the homeland, a pride he hasn't felt in quite some time. How sturdy they have made his armor! In fact, perhaps his friends are dead because during a break from their patrol, they took off their armor because of the heat. I am being baked like meat inside this can, Fernando had complained. That may be so, Brazo had admitted, but a man must suffer certain discomforts in order to survive. Why are we even here? Fernando had asked and they laughed cynically because they knew these free-roamers of the high desert wouldn't last a day inside mission walls. They break all the rules. Steal horses in the night, appear out of nowhere in surprise attacks, live on handfuls of food and water, scratch an existence out of nothing, and yet hold to that existence without complaint. He told Fernando he admired them for that, and Fernando said he agreed but still hated their guts for making his life miserable. Their discourse was interrupted by the sight of Cortazar, who was screaming and hopping around and clawing at himself, a scorpion underneath the armor. It prompted all the men, except Brazo, to strip whatever armor they still had left and ride on into the pass where they were ambushed and cut to pieces, all except Brazo.

He will grieve later for his friends, circumstances permitting, but the question arises of what to do now. Surrender? No, no good. Could they arrive at terms, a fair battle with just one? Difficult to convey this point of honor. Not good, not so good. Well then, he will advance, walk right through them. A larger contingent of soldiers is at camp, ten miles away, slow going on foot, almost impossible when hounded by men trying to kill him, but he takes a step in the direction of the camp, and then another. He can't help but pass the bodies of his friends. There is poor Fernando, his best friend ever since their training days in Spain. The gunky red mess of brains spill out from Fernandos's crushed skull. It comes to this, Fernando, it comes to this, your poor brains in the sand. He swallows hard but walks on. The Indios watch, startled, as if they were expecting him to stay in the circle of sand like a baited bear. He swings the long sword to clear the path.

Brazo begins to sing in a lively baritone, voice rumbling through the steel cage of his helmet, a ballad of lost men and cantina love, a sound startling in the high desert afternoon, now turning cooler. Perhaps they think he is a mad spirit, perhaps they are impressed by his courage, but the ambushers stand back and watch in amazement as Brazo marches past them.

Brazo clinks on. Step by step until he feels himself alone in the new world. It is a pretty land really, not all desert by any means, timbered in places, a shallow creek here and there, blue hills in the distance, not really so unlike the land around Grenada. Ah, Grenada!

He's bleeding. After all, a knife has found its way through the skirting of his armor, somewhere around his waist. He walks on, splashing blood with each agonizing step. Evening turns into long twilight, turns into night. The stars come out. The coyotes howl in the hills. He hears shuffling sounds somewhere behind him. Perhaps the Indios have returned, but he doesn't care. He will carry them in on his back if he needs. He will walk without blood if he needs. All he needs to do is step. One step at a time. Another. He violates his own rule now, takes his helmet off and tosses it aside. The night air rushes over his face. Delicious. Ah, truly, delicious. He tilts his chin to the stars. *Magnificent.* A star shoots across the sky. He has not noticed the stars in a long time, truly noticed them like this, in their multitude. If he thinks about the stars, he does not think so much about the gaping pain in his side. He pictures himself with his friends. They will attend to his wounds, grieve with him over the loss of Fernando and the others, and at the campfire in the night, the understanding will come that they are only pawns in the great show, unnamed stars in a vast universe, and they will offer each other what comfort they can, knowing it will be a long time, maybe forever, until any of them crosses the ocean back to home.

In this night so dark, he staggers toward a light still far in the distance. He reaches out an iron-gloved hand and calls for help, only a dry whisper now. His knees buckle. As he falls, an image arises in Brazo's mind, himself, many months before, first stepping onto a tropical shore, far to the south, legs wobbly from the sea, a rush of wind, a sultry mist in the air, a torrent of bird song and the scent of strange new flowers. He raises his sword to the sky, his great sword as yet unbloodied. Sunlight catches the sword, shafts of light bounce off the finest steel as he proclaims *I have come. It is I; it is Brazo!*

THE KINDNESS OF STRANGERS

As I put my pharmaceutical pouch back into my carry-on and wait to board the airplane, a heavy-set man with blotchy skin plops down beside me and I immediately sense he is an over-bearing person because at this late hour there is plenty of room in the boarding area for him to keep some distance between us. But he is one of those people who needs to talk, to say whatever he has on his mind, especially if he's caught on to something he can hold over you. He turns sideways and says with a chuckle, "I saw you were taking Beano. For the farts! Hey, I know, been there! Don't know what I would do without it!" He laughs and slaps his hand down on my thigh as if we are suddenly bonded, suddenly buddies.

I stare straight ahead.

He leans over and bumps his shoulder against mine. Chortles, eager for us to joke together. "Maybe we'd better not sit together, huh?"

"Maybe not."

"Man, I used to gas my wife right out of the bed. How about you?" More hilarity, more leaning over, more jiggling and bumping of his shoulder against mine. "Or maybe she farts, too, huh, the both of you blasting away, that's the way it is with me and my wife."

I don't like people talking about my wife, especially strangers, especially anyone who never knew her. I might let it pass but my stomach is bothering me and I'm tired tonight after a rough assignment

The final boarding call comes. I reach over to his shoulder. I do a little squeeze between his neck and shoulder, sort of like the Vulcan pinch of Dr. Spock, and he closes his eyes and slumps over in his seat as if deep into a most pleasant nap. But as a professional assassin, I am not so gentle or kind as Dr. Spock. The man will wake in a few hours with a tremendous headache. "Have a good trip," I say to my friend, and I hurry to board my plane.

THE LAKE, THE BLUE BLANKET

I don't recall now who called who, but it had been twenty years since we'd broken up, and I remember she sounded happy and wistful, which surprised me, and I felt happy and wistful to talk to her, too. We were both married and there was no going back but one thread of conversation led to another and I said, you know, it might have worked out, and she said oh please don't say that now. Then she said, but I remember the lake, and the blanket. A blue blanket, I said. And the places we found in the woods around the lake. She laughed. The things that went on on that blanket, she said, oh my, I recall that. I do too, I said, well, you've got somebody else now. It's not the same, she said, and there was that wistfulness in her voice. No, it's not the same, I said. The lake, she said, the blue blanket. The lake, I said. It's been another twenty years now and I guess there won't be another call, but sometimes at night I wake thinking about her, and the lake, and the blue blanket.

THE INTERVENTIONIST

The bare-handed fighter is at a distinct disadvantage when encountering an assailant with a knife or a gun. Some ask why I don't simply carry a gun or a knife myself. This is a good question, and I will attempt an answer. First off, I don't trust myself with a gun. I'm afraid I might shoot the wrong person or shoot someone unnecessarily. I am not a violent man and I seek no harm to my opponents: I only intervene by doing the minimum required, and it is very hard to do anything minimal with a gun. In Western movies, heroes are always shooting the gun hands of their enemies, who then wag their shot hand in the air as if the hand is wet. They might suck on it a little bit, and after a few moments, everybody's forgotten about the hand. Often, one doesn't even see any blood, as if the bullet has caromed off the wrist bone and left the gunslinger with a numbed but barely wounded hand. My own sense is that being shot in the hand would hurt like hell and the shot person would scream and hop around in pain. This isn't even to mention how good a shot one would have to be to aim at a hand and hit it. Another point, and a selfish one, is that I am afraid that if I owned a gun, I would just suddenly off myself one day. I'm often fairly cheerful, but I'm also pretty gloomy, and who knows what I might spontaneously do to myself on a bad day?

Well okay, then, what about a knife? Well, some of the same reasoning applies. Use a knife, and it's hard to just give a quick little nick. There the guy would be with a cut arm, bleeding like hell, screaming probably and hopping around. These things hurt like hell. It's not like in the movies. To tell the truth, I can't stand the thought of sticking someone with a knife. The whole idea makes me squeamish. I'd have to be in a really bad fix before I'd stab someone.

When I go into the woods on hikes, I carry a stick, a good stout stick, in case a mountain lion or a bear attacks. I have no idea how much good the stick will really do me, but it gives me some comfort. I can sort of picture myself hitting a lion with a stick. I'm not so sure about a bear. A bear would be an awfully big animal to hit with a stick. On the other hand, the alternative doesn't sound so good. Lie down and cover up and hope for the best. I'm not sure I would have the calmness of mind to do that. They always say not to turn and run. But I don't know. I think one might give it a go. Maybe throw the stick at the bear and haul ass.

One might wonder at this point who the hell am I? Some sort of nut? What I call myself is a Citizen's Interventionist. When I see a bad situation, someone needing help, I go in. I'm not fearless. I pick my shots. When at all possible, I call the cops. Sometimes I realize it's too much for me to handle and I clear out. There's some shame involved–sometimes I've been slow to act and slipped away or frozen up. I wouldn't rely on me.

WHAT ARE MY CHANCES

Dorothy sat on the other side of Mr. Jones's wide desk, clenching her hands in her lap as she awaited the editor's response to her most recent story. He had been rather brutal on the two before.

He wasn't a big man, but he had an intimidating presence. He didn't look old exactly, but he wasn't young. He was thin, graying, and wore thick glasses. "Your story is sweet," he said. "I was touched by your description of your grandfather in the nursing home, the way he tried to rise from his wheelchair, a trembling hand reaching toward you, as if he wanted to go after you, to go back into the world one last time."

"You really thought it was good?"

He frowned. "I said that it was sweet."

She leaned forward. "What do you think my chances are?"

In his vast chair, he sank away from her. "Your chances of what?"

"Of making it as a writer."

"Of making it as a writer?" His fingers were long and pale. With both hands, he touched them to the point of his chin. "I'd say your chances are practically zero." He tilted forward. "Bring me more of your stories. Not too often. Don't wear out your welcome."

She was determined to make it as a writer. To achieve fame. Well, no, not fame, she shouldn't even dream of that. *Respect.* To have her work respected, to have her stories thought to be, a little *important.* And yet that seemed so, so *egotistical.* And yet…She wrote a story about a writer, oh, somewhat like herself, certainly not *really* about herself, in which the young writer brooded about her future. She hoped Mr. Jones might consider the story thoughtful, yet shaded with a certain self-deprecating irony, perhaps even a very mild humor, though she didn't really get the whole comedy thing.

She dropped the story off at his office and a few days later he summoned her. He sat on the throne of his chair, the wide desk like a dangerous moat to be crossed. She rather liked those metaphors and she thought she might use them in a story one day if she ever dared to write about Mr. Jones.

He cleared his throat of the remains of a pretzel. He kept a large glass bowl of pretzels on a side table near the desk. She loved pretzels, but he never offered her one. His eyes darkened if he saw her glancing at the pretzels.

"Well, I'm afraid this one was a waste of my time. Your reflections about being a writer strike me as utterly vapid. Your writing isn't completely mindless, but it is not essentially of the mind."

Her face reddened, she stood up, her voice quaking like a guest whose shoes have been criticized for tracking mud. "I see. There's no point then…"

He rose too, and his voice softened. "I see you as a writer of the heart, and so I encourage you to leave the matters of the mind and go out and bring me a story that is sweet and tender, perhaps something about an orphan or a lost animal."

She left the office and on the bus home she almost started crying, but no, no damn it, she would write such a story. She would show the mean old bastard. She would break his heart with a story about a lost turtle.

For two weeks, she stayed up all night after working her shift at the diner, writing in her bedroom. She lived in a small apartment with her mother, who was nice, but who could be a real bruiser. In the night bruiser mom called out, "Stop writing! Go to sleep!"

She wrote and she rewrote, at home, on the bus to and from work, scribbling ideas on lunch tickets at the diner. Finally, her usually neat hair all in a frazzle, she dropped the story off. A week later, he called for her to come in.

He sat at the wide desk. Today the desk reminded her of nothing. It was just a big stupid desk. Her hands had been shaking for a week and she was given to sweating now, her brow sweating, the back of her dress stained with sweat. It was terrible, this writing thing, what it did to a person. What she most wanted now, after all the hard work, was a pretzel. But today the glass bowl was nowhere in sight.

He frowned as he held the edges of her manuscript as if it were something fragile that might tear between his fingertips.

"So there Tommy the turtle is, in its shell, the corners chipped and torn from a dog mauling, the pathetic little tail nipped by a hawk...Working his way through Missouri, Kansas, I wasn't always sure about the geography. But where does Tommy belong? Where does poor Tommy the turtle belong? It was a little overdone, the sentiment made me queasy at times, but still...aren't we all searching for our home?"

He lowered his head and a tremble ran through his shoulders. When he looked up, his eyes glistened beneath his thick glasses. "Go and write your stories. Bring me no more."

"No more?"

"I've taken you as far as I can."

She straightened in her chair, squared her shoulders. "What do you think my chances are?"

His chin dipped and his glasses slid down his long nose. "Your chances of what?"

"Of making it as a writer."

"Your chances of making it as a writer?" He held her manuscript at arm's length and frowned at it as if he'd just discovered a typo. "I'd say practically zero." With a tilt of his head, his glasses slid back into place. He cleared his throat. "But better than some. Maybe better than most."

He bent over, reached behind his desk, and set before her the bowl of pretzels. Her eyes widening, she leaned forward. He watched her, daring her to take one.

IT'S FREE TODAY

My patient Ed is going on about how he resents his brother, a successful businessman. I nod and scribble in my pad: *jealousy*. I could have done well too if I'd gotten the breaks, Ed says and I add: *Bitterness*. I just feel like a loser sometimes. I add: *self-loathing*.

I sigh. I get it. I get it all too well.

Do you want to listen to some music, Ed?

Listen to music?

Why not? Instead of me telling you stuff you probably already know, or stuff I've probably said a hundred times before, how about if I put on a nice piece of music and we just listen to it for a couple of minutes? Because to tell you the truth, I don't know what to tell you anymore and I thought we might just sit here together, or you could lie down on the couch if you want and we'll listen to the music.

I'm paying for this?

It's a freebie today, Ed, a freebie. I just don't have anything to tell you. I'm experiencing the same thing: jealousy, bitterness, self-loathing.

You are?

I am. I'm completely used up. I used to be a drunk. Did you know that?

He sits up straighter. Why no, I didn't know that.

And my wife just left me.

Man, I'm sorry to hear that.

Yeah, it's bad. As soon as you leave, I'll probably go down

to a bar and get roaring drunk.

Wow, Doc, I don't know what to say. Anything I can do for you?

Let's just sit here and listen to the music.

Sure, whatever you say.

Ed's the last patient today. No one else is coming. I turn off the light so that we sit in the gloom of evening. The branches of a tree scratch against the upstairs window of my office.

I shut my eyes. Something classical plays, with sounds in the background, dolphins or something talking, high-pitched sounds of creatures reaching out to each other. After a few minutes, Ed's chair squeaks with his rising, and he closes the door quietly on his way out. I'll just sit here for a while and breathe and listen to the music until I feel more like a person who might have someone waiting for him somewhere.

PROFESSOR SULLIVAN DISCOVERS THE FORCE

Professor Sullivan's thoughts are grim. He's anxious, wound tight. His wife gets him into a yoga class to loosen him up, but when he can't touch his toes, the instructor thinks he's a loser.

He doesn't know what to make of his family anymore. He hardly sees his two teenage sons. When their paths cross in the hallway, they scurry from him, ducking into their rooms, slamming their doors, turning their music loud as he stands outside the door, head pressed to the wood.

As he crosses campus on a snowy winter's morning, the revelation hits Professor Sullivan like a thunderbolt: everyone thinks he's a loser. How could he have gotten it so wrong for so many years? Why had he thought that people liked him, respected him even? Why hadn't he noticed before what everyone was really thinking?

His hands tremble. Coffee slogs over the rim of his carrying cup and splashes his tie. He continues his campus crossing, noting the disparaging expressions of the students hustling past him on the icy sidewalks. A muscular student knocks against his shoulder as he passes, sending Professor Sullivan's coffee cup sailing into the air.

As he enters his classroom and sets his briefcase down on his desk, the students slog back in their chairs and roll their eyes and send text messages.

As he opens his briefcase, he looks out at the flat-eyed students and his legs wobble. He pauses. He takes a breath.

He looks at them harder, blinks his eyes. They're a scruffy looking lot. He stares back with the same flat-eyed expression they're giving him. A rush of energy starts in his low back and flows up his spine and rises, hotly, to the top of his head. His eyes brighten. He feels himself grow taller. His chest expands. The students pause in mid-text message. His face glows with golden light. He flings his briefcase into the crowd, papers showering over the students. As they stare, astounded, he charges them, grabbing hold of a squirming kid by the sweatshirt, dragging him into the corridor. He gives him the bum's rush all the way out the front door of the building and pitches him out on the lawn. He comes back for another, but now they're scuttling away in all directions.

He becomes legendary. Through winter and into flowery spring, he hides in the high weeds by the pond. He springs out, waving his arms as students and former colleagues cry out in panic. He cackles madly as they flee before him.

THE MEDITATION MASTER

As I knelt on my pillow, through lidded eyes I noted the big bald meditation master walking in my direction, bamboo cane in hand, his long robe swishing and his slippers making a shuffling sound on the hardwood floor. On this weekend meditation retreat, he had already whacked me twice across the back with his cane, though others had suffered even more. We were all wondering what we'd gotten into. It wasn't a Buddhist retreat, it wasn't Christian, nobody knew quite what it was, but there we were, twenty or so meditators, come here to a quiet valley to work on our demons.

It was supposed to be a silent retreat, but there'd been some subtle muttering at lunch over thin soup and dry biscuits. The meditation master had sat at one end of a long cafeteria table, staring straight ahead as if we didn't exist, while we eyed him in trepidation. After lunch, a couple of our smarter ones whispered good bye and good luck, gathered their things and dashed for the parking lot.

We knelt in rows, with gaps between us so the meditation master could slide past us. As he came sidelong, I felt his presence at my side, with my peripheral vision glimpsed his black robe. I flinched inside, though I hoped no emotion, no thought registered on my face. I prayed he would pass me by, zero in on another target. He shuffled on, and I took a deeper breath. He turned about. There was a deadly silent pause as I held my breath, and then he whacked me across my back and shoulders, harder than the other times.

The blow stung. It enflamed my bad shoulder.

I'd taken it the other times, but this time I turned my head. From that angle, I could only see up to his knees. "Why did you do that?" I asked over my shoulder.

"You were thinking."

"I wasn't thinking very much."

He whacked me again. "Silence."

I've always had anger issues, one of the reasons I came here, to deal with those. I stood up and faced him. He was a big man, but soft matronly breasts pushed against his robe.

"If you hit me again, we're going to have a problem," I said.

"This isn't about you," he said, "This is your ego talking. We need to kill your ego." He spoke quietly, glancing around, as if he wanted to keep this between us. The others looked down, pretending to meditate.

"Maybe I'd better keep my ego. It's not much, but it's all I've got."

His eyes glinted. He swung the cane at my side. I blocked it and lowered my shoulders and drove my fist into his soft gut. He bent over, gasping. I ripped the cane from his hand. "Kneel down," I ordered. I pushed him down on the pillow while he sucked for air. "You need to lighten up," I said.

From somewhere to my left, a voice muttered, "Kick his ass" and a ripple of assent drifted through the dim meditation room.

I called out, "Settle down, boys."

Near the outside door, a tall skinny guy with long hair stood and tossed his pillow in the air. Now others stood and threw their pillows too.

"Now, fellows, easy," I said, but they were all on their feet now, bashing at each other with pillows, laughing like madmen. I became aware of the cane in my hand, had a sudden urge to lash out, to bring them back into control.

The skinny long-haired guy suddenly screamed "Run!" I swung my head around, noticing the empty pillow where the master had been kneeling moments before, then took in the sight of what had caused the panic. "Whoa!" I cried out, "run!"

The meditation master had come out of a side room carrying a long sword, a kind of scimitar. Everyone bolted, fighting to get out the door like fans at a soccer riot. We scattered into a golden light, some dodging into the trees, others dashing for the parking lot. I looked back. He didn't run after us, but he moved nimbly for a fat man in a long robe. I ran for the red brick dorm. I ran up the stairs to my room and moments later the door to the building opened. His slippers slid up the stairs one by one. There was no lock on the door. I dug in my suitcase.

He pushed through the door, came in like a rush of wind. I whirled around. He stood holding the sword with two hands. I aimed my policeman's .38 special at his chest.

He frowned, noting the gun. "You have a bad attitude," he said.

"I know. I've always had a bad attitude. That's why I came here."

He made a sighing sound in his throat, a sigh that spoke of longstanding disappointment in the shabby crew of meditators with bad attitudes who had found their way here to this quiet valley. "We'll continue your training another time," he said. "When you have more receptivity."

"I look forward to it. But for the moment, you have the right to remain silent."

He took a deep breath, the sort of steadying breath one takes before facing the judge. He dropped the sword and I stepped behind and cuffed the meditation master.

WAKE ME WHEN IT'S OVER

Samuels came out of the tent in the Serengeti and realized his wife Julie had taken off in the jeep with his best friend Lyle, who was also their guide on this trip for some reason that didn't make sense because Lyle didn't know any more about Africa than they did. But here he was, their guide. Though Lyle was handsome in a goofy sort of way, with his droopy walrus moustache, it was hard to see why Julie had fallen for him, but there'd been nights around the campfire when he'd caught them staring at each other, then glancing furtively at him. Now his suspicions were confirmed. No jeep and they had left him to die with many miles to cross in this lion-infested, waterless, barren land.

He did the sensible thing, of course, which was to realize he would need to bond with nature, go wild to survive, and so he took off all his clothes except his underwear, walked a few feet, winced, realized his mistake, so put back on his boots and set off at a good pace. Now just up ahead a lion rose from the grass, and now another, and he walked on, and now there were more lions. He started to run but within moments they pounced on him and tore him to shreds with hyenas already moving in and dragging off body parts, thought it seemed he was watching from a distance now, that it was someone else's body that was being ripped to shreds. Heart pounding, Samuels woke now in his comfy bed in the city with Julie beside him and he was sweating and breathing quickly, and it took him a few moments to settle down. He was a little angry at Julie even though he was relieved to know this was all a dream and what would she see in Lyle anyway? It was ridiculous to imagine anything between them, even if Lyle did come over quite a bit, maybe a little more than one might expect. But after all they had been best friends for many years, long before Julie had come into his life.

"What is it?" Julie asked, rolling over. "What's wrong?" It always bothered her when he woke in the night. She said it kept her from falling back to sleep herself.

"I had a dream," he said. He told her about the dream. He chuckled and said, "You and Lyle, silly isn't it?"

Julie was silent. Then he heard her quiet breathing. "It's not so silly."

"What?"

"We didn't know how to tell you. I'm leaving you for Lyle," she said in that brusque way she sometimes had.

Samuels bolted up in bed. Julie was still sleeping, snoring slightly but firmly in that lovely sort of way she had of snoring. My God, he realized, it's one of those *double dreams*. It's one of those dreams where you thought you'd woken up but you were actually still dreaming. He was afraid to go back to sleep right way so he rose, put on his bathrobe, and went into their living room. They lived in a condo on the ninth floor, the highest floor in the building. He slid open the glass door and stepped out on the small terrace, closing the door behind him. He looked out on the lights of the city, spreading out, so pretty, and he could see the river in the distance, the way the lights glimmered off the water. He loved the wind up high where they lived, blowing his hair, making his eyes moisten, bringing him back to his senses.

He heard a noise and turned to see Julie sliding open the door, slender and lovely in her nightgown. Julie, the light and love of his life. It seemed a miracle that they had found each other, both of them so searching and lost when they first met until they found happiness together. Well, happiness most of the time anyway, more than he'd ever known before. Maybe he was inclined to moods, but she'd brought out the best in him. She stood beside him at the railing which came to their waists.

"What's wrong?" she asked.

He told her about the double dream. She held her nightgown to her throat and her head ducked down and away, and she looked out at the lights of the city, but not at him. "It's not such a strange dream...Look, it hasn't been right between us for a long time now, you know that."

A burning sensation rose in his throat. "What are you talking about? I thought things were great."

"That's the problem, isn't it? You never understand anything."

"What are you saying?"

"It just happened, okay. I didn't mean it to happen. Lyle's fun to be with. It's always depressing with you. You're gloomy all the time. Is it so wrong to want a little happiness in my life?"

He stared at her and then he laughed.

"What?" she said. "Why are you laughing like that? You sound weird."

"A triple dream," he said, still laughing. "It's a triple dream. That beats all."

She was moving away toward the sliding glass door

when he grabbed her wrist and pulled her to the railing. "Come here."

"I don't want to. Let me go."

He tilted back against the railing, holding her to his chest as she struggled. The lights of the city spun around his head. "It's just a dream," he said, laughing. She fought him, broke free of him as they went over.

She screamed and clawed at the air and kicked her feet. He went down smoothly, his hands up, the lights of the city dazzling and beautiful. He knew you always woke up before you hit the ground.

TRUMP TEACHES MY WRITING WORKSHOP

This is great. Fantastic to be here. We all know why we're here. Why are we here? To talk about Carl's story? Is it Carlo? From Cuba? Can I call you Carlo? Carl, from Michigan? Irish? What the hell kind of name is Carl? Isn't that a hamburger? Where the hell are you from, Carl? Forget it. I love your story. I haven't read it. But this first line is beautiful. 'The moon…" I love that, 'the moon', I mean who the hell wouldn't love that? What about Mars? Mars, the moon, work it out. But this next part, I don't know, 'rose over…' Rising, falling, who cares You're losing me here. We need more energy, this is low energy, this rising, falling stuff. Move the story to Cuba, that's what I'd do. The beard. What was wrong with the other guy? Put them in a room, work it out, make a deal. Nobody makes good deals. The thing with the Brits? What the hell was that all about? Put them in a room. King George, Washington, Ben Franklin–now there was a guy! Put them in a room, work it out, make a deal. I could do it in ten minutes. It would be easy. King George played us–he wanted to unload. He took us for a ride. I mean what the hell, we don't even get a castle? You fight a war, you ought to at least get a castle. You got to take the castles. Or the wigs. Take the wigs. Was the king even British? He played us like babies.

We need more energy in Carlo's story. Forget the moon. Try this. Let's say Little Carlo is Castro's buddy. Little Carlo finds out a big secret. Castro's got one nuke left. He's been hiding it all these years. He's going to hit Miami. It's up to Carlo to stop him. He's a genius or something. What's with the kids these days? They're all computer geniuses, I don't know. They got their little boxes. They punch their little buttons. It's great. Anyway, Carlo rigs it so that the nuke falls into the ocean. He saves millions of people, Carlo, he's a hero. Does he die? I don't know. It's your story, Carlo. It's beautiful. Lose the moon. Set it on Mars. You don't look Irish to me.

KIOWA JIM IS HERE

Lefty goes out to check the horses and runs back into the cabin a minute later, crying out, "Kiowa Jim! I saw Kiowa Jim!"

We all jump up, grabbing our guns. All of us except Whiskey Ed, who just sits at the table, dealing solitaire, a smirk on his face. "You're crazy," he says. "Kiowa Jim doesn't ride this far north."

"I saw him! I saw Kiowa Jim. Out by the horses."

"Are you sure?" I ask.

"It was him. It was Kiowa Jim."

Lefty's usually a reliable man. "Make sure you're loaded, boys," I say. "Pistols, your rifles, too. Put a knife in your belt."

Mesquite Pete's prone to overreact and he says in a quavering voice, "He'll kill us all. He'll take our nuts while we're still alive. That's what he does."

Whiskey Ed snorts. "You ever see him do that?"

"Sure I have. I heard about it."

Yukon Jack's eyes are wild. "Mad beaver!" he cries out.

"What the hell are you talking about?" I ask.

"I seen it! Beaver gone mad. Rabies! Hundreds of them. Drag a man down!"

"Shut up. Nobody here's getting killed by a mad beaver or by Kiowa Jim. There's five of us. We've got the door barred. We'll wait him out."

"He'll burn us out," Pete says. "That's what he does. He'll burn down the cabin and shoot us down like dogs when we come out."

Whiskey Ed pulls on his bottle. "You ever seen him do that? Burn down a cabin and shoot people when they come out?"

"Sure I have. I heard about it."

We hear stirring out by the corral, the horses moving, kicking their hooves around, something swinging out there, metal against wood. The wind picks up, rattles the cheap plank boards of the cabin. I look at the walls. This place would go up like tinder. Whiskey Ed's noticing the same thing, frowning at the walls. He pushes his bottle away and stands up. "Turn out the lamp."

We stand in the darkness, listening to our breathing. "I don't like this," Whiskey says. "If he is out there, I don't like the idea of waiting to be burned out."

"What are you suggesting?"

"Let's try talking to him. Open the door a crack. Talk out to him. Find out what he wants. Negotiate."

"He wants our nuts," Lefty says. "How do you negotiate with a guy like that?"

"Mad beaver!" Yukon Jack screams. His big body barrels around in the darkness and we grab him and hold him.

"Shut up!"

He writhes and flings his arms about, but he settles when Ed pours a long drink down his throat.

But now Mesquite Pete's losing it. "Oh, just kill me!" he sobs, "I can't stand this waiting. Just kill me and get it over with!"

It's tempting, but I say, "Shut up, Pete. I'm going to open the door. You all stand behind me. Whatever happens, don't let him grab me."

The boys huddle behind me as I crack open the door. "Kiowa Jim! We've got no quarrel with you!"

No response. Just the sound of the wind. The horses stirring.

"What do you want with us?" I shout.

Lefty's behind me, pressed into my back by the others. I can't still my beating heart.

"He wants one of us!" Mesquite Pete screams. "Take Lefty!" He shoves Lefty by me, and I don't try to grab him as he stumbles past into the darkness. I bar the door while Lefty turns about and beats at the wood and pleads to be let in.

"Go fight him like a man!" Whiskey Ed yells through the door.

Lefty screams and we hear running; maybe he's looking for cover in the darkness. Then there are more terrified screams. Something heavy falls against the door. Lefty's back, whimpering, "Let me in! Please let me in."

"Aim your guns at the door," I say.

"We're going to shoot Lefty now?" Whiskey asks. "That doesn't seem right."

"Not Lefty. If Kiowa Jim tries to come in, shoot him."

I open the door, grab Lefty by the shirt, drag him in and he falls on the plankwood floor.

Mesquite Pete is frantic. "Did he take your nuts?"

"I don't think so," Lefty blubbers.

"Better check him, Whiskey."

Whiskey bends over him. "He's good."

"He'll burn us out!" Mesquite Pete yells.

"Okay, we're going to make a break for it," I say. "Stick together. Guns ready. We'll get the horses and ride out. He can't kill us all."

We move through the darkness. The wind in our hair. The horses stirring. Our labored breath. "Stay low," I whisper.

"Keep your wits about you," Whiskey encourages.

"There he is!" Mesquite Pete screams.

"I see him!" Lefty cries back.

Yukon Jack, huge and wild-eyed, rears up before me. "Mad beaver!"

Then we're all firing at once, shot after shot, spinning around, firing into the darkness. Something takes the breath out of me. Right in the middle, up high in the chest. I'm flat on the ground, the stars overhead, the horses out of the corral now and running. I hear a couple more shots and then silence. Bodies lie sprawled around me. I call out, "Boys?" Only one slow voice calls back, "I'm here," but I can't even get my head to turn his way.

"You hit, Whiskey?"

"Yeah," he calls slowly. "I guess I am. I'm hit real good."

"I am too."

We lie there in the darkness for a while. He gives a tired sort of chuckle, and I know he's thinking how much he'd like a last pull on the bottle. "Well, at least we can say it was Kiowa Jim that got us."

The stars brighten over our heads. Brightest I've ever seen them. Or maybe I haven't noticed them in a long time. "No," I say, "We can't even say that."

AFTER ZOMBIES

When I answered my phone this morning, my agent Burt screamed in my ear, "What comes after zombies? What comes after zombies?"

"I don't know," I said, "I don't know."

For weeks, we've been racking our minds over how to catch the next literary wave. We're sick of being poor, of barely hacking it. The only thing sadder than a failed writer is a failed agent.

My wife called out from the kitchen where she was burning up the oatmeal, "Is it Burt? Has he sold something?"

"No, he hasn't sold anything. But we're close."

"We're always close!" She went back to burning the oatmeal.

"What comes after zombies?" I shouted at her.

"Killer squirrels!" she shouted.

"Killer squirrels!" I screamed at Burt.

He paused. "Pitch it to me."

"Okay, look. Everything appears normal. A man goes out on his deck with his paper and a cup of coffee. Nice summer morning. His wife is inside burning up the oatmeal. The kids are at the parole office. He watches the squirrels in the trees. Cute. Wow, what jumpers! Look at them go, one branch to another...But something is wrong. Something is terribly wrong."

"What is it?"

"The squirrels are devouring something big. Something really big..."

"Like what?"

"Like a...like a deer. They've dragged a deer up into the trees and they're devouring it."

He breathed heavily. "How many squirrels are there?"

"Well, it started as a few, but now, it's hundreds, thousands. They're leaping over the fence. Now they finish the deer and start for the man."

"No. No, it's been done. Hitchcock. The Birds. Same old stuff, but with squirrels."

"Burt doesn't like the killer squirrels!" I called to my wife.

"Tell Burt to shove it!" She came to the doorway, waving a big wooden spoon. "Tell him to sell something or shove it!"

"What's she saying?" Burt said. "What's she saying?"

"She says to try a little harder."

"I'm trying! You've got to give me something. You've got to feed me, baby, you've got to feed me."

"Killer babies!"

"Pitch it. Make me believe it."

"Little Oscar's in his crib. Mama reaches in, lifts little Oscar, warm and fuzzy music now, opens her dress to breastfeed... Kid goes for her jugular, blood everywhere, daddy comes in, screams, too late for him too."

Burt hesitated, and then said, "No, no. It's just a mix of vampires and Jaws."

"Jaws ...A sad story about a man who can't chew anymore."

"He's lost his teeth?"

"No...He's faced with a moral dilemma. He's a scientist.

He's produced a kind of technology, sort of like an x-ray that reveals that the air is full of little human beings flying through the air, microscopic human beings, but with the machine he can see them clearly and whenever he opens his mouth the little men and women fly into his mouth, screaming, so if he chews, he will be eating the little human beings."

Burt made a sniffling sound. "Yuck," he moaned. "Serious yuck."

My wife stood in the doorway holding a big wooden spoon. "What's he saying now?"

"He says we need a new angle."

She waved her spoon and went away again.

"Burt?" I said. "Burt? Do you think I should just go back to writing poetry?"

"You're killing me, baby, you're killing me." Then I heard it. The sound that always sends chills through me. He was beating his phone against his head. Tap, tap, tap, beat beat, knock.

"Alien vampire squirrels!" my wife shouted from the kitchen.

"Alien vampire squirrels," I said.

The knocking paused. He took a breath. "Go on."

My wife stood in the doorway. Her spoon was covered in oatmeal. "Well?"

"He loves it!"

THE WAY TO HANDLE BULLIES

Just because you asked, let me tell you about myself. I am sixty-three years old. Five-foot five and a hundred and fifty pounds of kick-ass muscle. Maybe I don't have what they call a six-pack, my stomach muscles don't show off like that, but they are strong beneath the surface. And the arms? Oh man, veins up and down the biceps and forearms. Incredible.

When you are short, bigger people sometimes think that they can bully you. When this happens, I have several techniques I use, but one is something I picked up in the fourth grade from Sister Bernadette. I grab hold of an ear and start pulling as hard as I can. Big grown men cry for mercy as I lead them around a barroom and kick them in the ass and out the door. If they come back in, I go for the other ear. Another technique is to lie down on the floor and start kicking like crazy, at shins, kneecaps, the groin. Or I'll spring off my toes and leap around a man's neck, wrap my legs around his waist like a boa constrictor and bite the end of his nose. Sobers the biggest bully right up.

I don't use weapons, not guns or knives. I hit Big Eddie in the head with a bottle once. We were at a party and Big Eddie got very out of line and was a danger to himself and others and so after he punched his wife, who was short and squat and wearing a long brown coat even though the apartment was hot, I picked up a bottle from a table and smashed it over his head. It was terrible. It was not like in the movies. He didn't crumple up into a nice helpless unconscious heap on the floor. No. Big Eddie cried out,

"Ow! Ow!" like a kid hurt on the playground and he went stumbling around the party holding his head while everyone stared at Big Eddie holding his head and lurching around and then all the party-goers were staring at me, the guy holding the bottle and then the blood started coming down over his forehead and someone asked, What happened to Big Eddie, and Big Eddie's wife, who looked very wide and formidable in that long brown coat, pointed at me and said with great venom, "Chuck hit him! Chuck hurt my husband!" And there I was with the bottle in my hand and suddenly Big Eddie was the victim and I was the bully. So I would be very hesitant to ever hit someone over the head with a bottle ever again. I don't like being the bully. I love everyone, really. Even Big Eddie. Especially Big Eddie Can't we all just love?

SOMEONE ELSE

They were watching. They would check him out first, to see if he would put up a fight. He was a small man, but well-muscled, a martial arts expert. Well, maybe not exactly an expert. But he had taken some classes. He was tough. He would fight them off or die trying. He would not be broken.

They were in the chow line, standing before the steaming oatmeal. The large man behind him pressed closer so that their trays bumped together. The man's hand reached out and touched him on the ass. The hand didn't squeeze, just rested there. He swivelled and the hand moved away. He gave the man The Look, modeled after various actors. His eyes narrowed, turned glinty and cold and deadly, his mouth almost smiling. "Easy, Governor," he said. Nice and smooth. Easy, Governor, that was good. The big man's eyes fell flat, and they accepted their scoops of gray oatmeal, picked up their juices and moved away in different directions.

In the shower, he turned his face up to the water. He would only have three minutes to shower, but the warm spray felt wonderful and purifying and he was determined to appreciate the small things to help him survive. Those to the left and right of him had moved on and for a moment, he felt a delicious sense of solitude. Then the arm came around his neck and tightened, pulling his head back at a painful angle. He thrust back with his elbow and it hit something solid and the man behind grunted, but the arm did not release. He fought, tried to fight, but there were three or four of them now and they brought him to the wet floor. Other arms went under his stomach, held him up. They propped up his knees and spread them. Nobody spoke. He opened his mouth to scream for the guard, but the arm around his throat was choking him out.

As he faded out, he reached over his shoulder, dug his fingers into a man's hair, flipped him neatly over his back. He sprang to his feet and pushed the other men against the walls of the shower.

He discovered himself lying alone, his cheek on the cool wet tile, curled up and holding his stomach, until he became aware of the guard's black shoes in front of his eyes. "Get up," the guard said. When he didn't, the guard gave him a light kick in the ribs with the toe of his shoe, and then again when he didn't rise. Pain went through his body, stirring him, and he pulled himself to a knee. "Get up," the guard said, not unkindly now. "Be smart. Go along to get along."

When he rose, at first his steps were slow and shuffling, and it felt as if he were dragging someone else's body through the steamy shower. His hands shook as he dressed. But with each step, his walk became more certain, and now as he strode past the rows of cages, his arms created waves of energy as men cowered and fell away from him on all sides.

THE WRONG CALL

Richardson and his wife sat on the deck, eating their dinner, looking out on their back yard. It was not a big yard, but the oak trees provided a pleasant shade. He liked the smell of the newly cut grass, and the yard looked good to Richardson after his afternoon mowing. Margaret had not commented on his mowing. Sometimes she did. Sometimes she said, "The yard looks very nice," or something to that effect.

To their right, though they could not see them because of the hedges at the fence line, the neighbors were laughing and shouting and splashing around in their pool. There were always many kids over there and probably some grandkids. The neighbors were always having a fine time. It was not really the sort of neighborhood where one would expect to find a swimming pool, and Richardson thought the pool a bit ostentatious.

He and Margaret had been married for many years, and the children were grown now and moved away. Sometimes one dropped by. Sometimes one called. Then they might not hear from them for weeks.

His steak was okay, but not great. He had cooked it himself, though, on the grill, and even made the barbecue sauce himself, so he could not really complain about it to Margaret. Usually she came out and looked over his shoulder as he grilled and said something encouraging, but this evening she had just disappeared inside, making a salad. "How's your steak?" he asked.

She looked at him as if it were a startling question. Her mouth was dabbed with barbecue sauce.

"Good," she said. "It's good."

He poked at his salad with his fork. "The salad seems a little oily."

She set her fork and knife down. She looked long at him. "Actually, the meat is a little tough tonight."

"A moment ago you said it was good."

She picked up her fork and knife and sawed at the meat. She was really working her elbow and shoulder, as if she were sawing a piece of lumber. "Good," she said, "but a little tough."

They went on eating. He listened to the laughter of the neighbors. Probably they really weren't even in the pool. They were just standing around shouting and laughing so that the neighbors would think they were having a good time.

He cleared his throat. "You know, you haven't said much all day. You aren't very good company right now."

She stared at him. "Is that right? Well, you're not very good company, either. "

As they continued eating, he stole glances at her. Her face looked a little red.

"What kind of facial lotion are you using these days?" he asked.

"What?" she said, "*What*?"

"Your face looks a little splotchy or something."

She threw down her napkin. She went inside. He heard her on the phone, talking in a loud voice.

He came in. "Who are you talking to?"

"My cousin Beth. I'm going to visit her."

He frowned and glanced up at the ceiling. It looked like it could use a new paint job. That might be something he and Margaret could tackle soon. He could paint while she held the ladder and kept the brushes clean. He looked back at her.

"I thought your cousin Beth was dead."

"She's not dead!"

He scratched at his head. "Where the heck has she been?"

"Oh, just go get a beer and watch some television."

"Well, okay."

He got a beer out of the fridge and started watching a ball game. After a while, he started feeling pretty good. This was okay. Drinking a beer, watching a ball game. But the rest of the house was too quiet. "Margaret?" he called. He might not always want to talk, but he liked knowing she was somewhere around. Also, he could not find the remote control.

A runner slid into home plate and the umpire called him out. Richardson disagreed with the call. The announcers also disagreed. They replayed the moment, the ball smacking into the catcher's glove, the runner starting his slide, his cleats throwing up a cloud of dirt, the catcher pivoting his shoulders and lowering the glove a fraction of a second behind the runner's shoe snaking over the plate.

The manager ran out of the dugout and argued about the call. Richardson was backing the manager here; no doubt about it, the runner was safe. The manager stuck his chin out and hollered. The umpire stood with his legs wide. The manager kicked dirt on the umpire's shoes. The umpire rocked back, wound his body up, and jerked his thumb toward the stands. *You're out of here!* The manager raised his eyes to the sky, spread his hands in disbelief, an innocent victim of an unjust system. Richardson swore at the umpire.

He got another beer. This was great stuff. He wanted to replay it for Margaret. He liked to call her over and replay things. He needed to find the remote and she was good at finding it. She was good at a lot of things.

"Margaret!" he called into the empty house. "Margaret!"

ON THE INTERNET THIS MORNING

On the internet this morning, I learn that the exercises I've been doing for years will not make me leaner or stronger but will most likely injure or debilitate me and make me softer and fatter and probably shorter too. I've also been screwing up on the dental end; my gums will rot, my teeth will fall out. The supplements I'm taking are loaded with lead. I've been ignoring some very bad warning signals. I may be going blind or be subject to sudden seizures or a stroke. Moving on from health, I learn that my financial planning is utterly foolish and immoral. Crime is rising in my state and our congressman is indicted. My favorite restaurant is closing. A fine Saturday morning is just beginning and all is well.

MR. O'BRIEN'S LAST SOLILOQUY

We came back from the war and we were just rolling along for a while, all through the fifties, like there was nothing but good times ahead. One of my happiest memories is standing in dirt. The good dirt in our back yard. Our new house. We'd had a smaller house but now there was another kid on the way and we got the new big house. Everything felt new. The whole neighborhood was new. Brick houses. Ranch mostly. But all of them a little different. Not like today.

We'd pitch the colichee over the back yard into the alley. All of us. Mary, me, the kids. It was something we did together. We pitched it over the fence. Cleaning it out so the grass would grow. All of us in the yard and throwing the lumps of colichee over the fence. Standing in the dirt. In our backyard. Our home. There was something I did only when I was alone, after we got the kids to bed. I'd go out in the yard and I'd patrol it. I'd walk the fence line. Sometimes I lay down on the dirt, when it was dark in the yard and nobody could see me. I lay down in the dirt and I stared up at the stars and I said to myself, this is all right, this is mine.

We went to a school play once, when Len was in kindergarten. He had a role where he had some kind of magical dust sprinkled over him. He lay down on the stage. He was supposed to roll over now and then to show he was dreaming. But every time he rolled he got closer to the edge of the stage. There was a big drop-off, four or five feet or so. He kept getting closer to the edge. You couldn't tell whether it was part of the play or whether he really was asleep and he was going to roll right off the edge of the stage and break his neck. I was a wreck watching him get closer and closer. I almost jumped out of my seat.

The sixties came along and it was like the world blew up in our faces. The Bay of Pigs, the Cuban missile crisis, J.F.K. Right here in Texas. I heard things at the office. A couple of men I'd considered friends, men I'd liked, over at the water cooler, they were talking about how Kennedy got what he deserved, he couldn't come down here telling us what to do. I fired them. I fired both of them right on the spot. I told them to get the hell out of the store.

Then I sat in my office and I cried. I'd never fired anybody before, not unless they were stealing. He was our president. And in Texas. Right here. On our watch. It made me sick.

I thought it was Oswald acting alone. I don't know anymore. I don't know what to think. Mary never agreed with me. The C.I.A, she thought, the Mafia, Castro, the Ku Klux Klan, she would get these ideas in her head and she wouldn't let them go. He didn't act alone. She must have said that a thousand times until I wanted to tear my hair out.

I don't know why it upset me so much when she said he didn't act alone. I guess it was like, well, if he didn't act alone, who could you trust?

Everything was changing. The blacks and their marches. Mary said of course they're marching. Why shouldn't they march? I'd march too. I hired a Negro in the accounting department. He was the best man for the job, so I hired him. You'd have thought I turned a shark loose in the store. They hated him and they were mad at me for hiring him and I guess I was relieved when he came to me and said, I'm sorry, Mr. O'Brien, it's not working out for me here. Mary told me I should have stood up for him more. Mary was right about a lot of things. You never know things until it's too late.

I smoked like crazy back then. Mary did too. We all smoked. Why didn't it kill me the way it killed Mary? I wanted it to be me, not her, if it had to kill somebody. I knew I was supposed to quit. We all knew. That's baloney that we didn't know.

The bad things just kept coming. It was like you couldn't get over one thing before something else hit. Vietnam. Bobby Kennedy, Martin Luther King. The kids going wild. The hair, the drugs. My own sons, hair down to their asses. Why did it get on my nerves so much? I should have just let it go. And it's nothing compared to today. You see it all now—green hair, purple hair. Rings through the nose. The lips, the eyes. Nice looking black girl comes in to help me to the toilet the other day and she opens her mouth and she's got a silver hoop through her tongue. That's all new.

Len was a good kid. Sure, some trouble here and there, but a good kid. Then they called him up for his own war. One war in the family was enough. Mary told him he wasn't going. She was going to make him go to Canada. But what could we do? If I could do it again, I'd take him to Canada myself. You never know things until it's too late.

Everything's new. I'm not even sure if this is the same country we fought for. The other day I woke up and I thought: I don't even know if this is America anymore. Maybe this isn't a country at all anymore. In a real country, you've got a goal. You're got a purpose. You're working together. You're building for the future. You want to make the world a little better for your kids.

What's our purpose now? I'm not sure I see a purpose anymore. People are just walking around talking on cell phones and buying things or shouting at each other on the television.

If you asked me what I believed in, I'd say kids. Sure, kids. Your own kids, then you get the grandkids, now there's the great-grandkids. I can't keep them straight, who is who. I don't think they know who I am either, but my grandkids, and I'm not even sure about all their names either, push them at me and say, go give Pa-Pa a hug. I scare them, in my wheelchair, but I like the hugs. I'll take what I can get. Pa-Pa. I get a kick out of that.

I got so little time with my own kids. I was always working. When you are ninety-four years old, I will tell you one thing you will not regret. You will not regret that you didn't work more. It's always too late. By the time you know anything, it's too late. Maybe you can warn people not to make the same mistakes. Not that they'll listen. But here it is, if you want to hear it.

Don't work so damn hard. Spend more time with your kids. And throw your kid in a closet and tie him up before you let him go off and get killed in a war. Because in the end you're the only one who will care. You and your family. The country will survive without your kid. You're the only one who will miss him every day for the rest of your life.

I didn't expect all these years to keep running by. After Mary went, I wanted to follow. But the heart keeps beating, the lungs keep breathing. It's a new day, a whole new ballgame. What's with all the machines to keep you alive? What's the point? There comes a time to call it quits, bag it in.

Time. I wouldn't want to be young again. One time through is enough. I wouldn't mind being eighty. I was still going strong at eighty. I walked five miles a day. But if I was eighty, I'd be missing Mary all over again. After she went, I tried to walk away the pain or it was like I wanted the pain to be somewhere else, to be in my hips or my back or my feet, anywhere but the pain eating away inside.

Funny, Mary is closer to me again. I can't explain it, but I see her a lot now. That girl with the hoop in her tongue rolled me into the bathroom and I saw her in the mirror, standing behind my chair, and for a minute she looked just like Mary, different color and all, but she still looked like Mary, and I said, Mary, just like that, Mary, and she bent over and she hugged me and she said, that's okay, honey, that's okay now.

WHEN I CAN'T SLEEP

When I can't sleep, I lie in bed and think about old lovers of mine, but that soon becomes depressing. I think of jobs I've had, the people I knew at every job, the people I'd liked, the ones I'd laughed with, the ones I hadn't liked so well. Then I try to picture every place I have ever lived, visualizing every room, the front door, the hallways, the bathrooms, the sinks in the bathrooms, the tub. Then I think of all the trips I have ever taken, starting at the latest and working my way backwards, and when I arrive in Tulsa, Oklahoma at the age of twelve, that's the one that puts me out.

ABOUT THE AUTHOR

Robert Garner McBrearty's award-winning short stories have appeared in over one hundred publications including in The Pushcart Prize, *Missouri Review*, *North American Review*, *New England Review*, *Witness*, *Narrative*, *StoryQuarterly*, and *Ellery Queen Mystery Magazine,* along with recent flash fiction publications in *Fiction Southeast, decomP*, *New Flash Fiction Review*, *the Café Irreal*, *Brilliant Flash Fiction*, *Eclectica*, *flashfiction.net* and elsewhere. As well, he's published three collections of short stories and a novella. He's received the Sherwood Anderson Foundation Fiction Award, a New Mexico State Arts Grant, the Wilda Hearne Flash Fiction Prize, fellowships to the MacDowell Colony and the Fine Arts Work Center in Provincetown, Massachusetts, and an adapted story took first place at the Maine Drama Festival. Currently, he teaches writing courses at Lighthouse Writers North in the Denver area.